Magic of the Black Mirror

by Ruth Chew

Illustrations by the author
Cover art by Rudy Nappi

A
LITTLE APPLE
PAPERBACK

SCHOLASTIC INC.

New York Toronto London Auckland Sydney

*To my grandson
Sven Mathiesen Jensen*

ISBN 0-590-43186-2

12 11 10 9 8 7 6 5 4 3 2 1   0 1 2 3 4 5/9

Printed in the U.S.A.   28

First Scholastic printing, April 1990

Magic of the Black Mirror

1

"COMING in here was a great idea, Mandy. It was awfully hot in the park." Will Corrigan looked around. "Wow! What a high ceiling!"

"Maybe that's why this room is so nice and cool," Amanda said.

Will walked over to a large glass case. "Look at these things."

His sister stared at a little fringed leather skirt in the case. For a minute she didn't speak. Then she said in a low voice, "Will, I just thought of something weird!"

"What do you mean?" her brother asked.

"Think about it, Will. Every one of these things belonged to an Indian long ago," Amanda told him.

Will scratched his head. "You're right. It. *is* kind of spooky. I guess that's a real moccasin next to the tomahawk over there." He turned and looked hard at his sister. "Mandy, did you know this stuff was here?"

Amanda grinned. "I thought you'd like it. We all did."

"You mean," Will said, "you've been to the Brooklyn Museum before?"

"Mrs. Coleman brought our class here last spring," Amanda told her brother. "Isn't it a great place?"

Will moved to the next case. "There's more Indian stuff here, but this is different."

"These things were made by another

set of Indians. They lived on the plains."
Amanda was two years older than Will.
It was fun to show off how much she
knew about Indians.

On one side of the room there were
five enormous wooden poles. They were
covered with carvings of birds and people
and animals, one on top of the other.
All the carvings had big eyes and big
beaks or mouths. Most of them had heads
that seemed too large for their bodies.

"Totem poles!" Will went over to look
at them.

Amanda ran after her brother.

Will was staring up at the totem poles.
Now something else caught his eye.
"Hey, look at those! Wow!" He ran to
the center of the room. Four giant wooden
statues stood on tall stands. The stands
were right in front of stone pillars that
reached to the ceiling.

Will climbed on the base of the nearest

pillar. From here he could see the top of a stand that held one of the wooden statues. "What do you know? There's a mirror here!"

Will leaned far over and looked down into the mirror. "Mandy, this is *really* weird!"

Her brother kept staring down into the mirror. Amanda climbed up beside him to see what was so interesting. "It's a black mirror," she said.

The mirror showed the beautiful carving on the statue's underside, but everything around the statue in the mirror seemed dark and strange. Amanda thought she could see trees and water. Suddenly the air smelled salty, and she could hear gulls screaming. It made her think of Coney Island.

Amanda took a deep breath and looked up. There was the big wooden statue, but it looked quite different now.

The statue wasn't old and cracked anymore. It was painted red and black and looked almost new. And there was no sign of the stone pillar.

Will grabbed his sister's arm. "Mandy," he whispered. "We're not in the museum anymore!"

2

SECRETLY Amanda was glad to have her brother beside her, but she didn't want him to know she was afraid.

"What's happened to us, Mandy?" Will asked.

Amanda thought hard. "Somehow we must have gotten into magic," she told him.

Will was quiet for a little while. Then he said, "I always thought magic would be fun, but it's scary."

Amanda looked around. High overhead sea birds were flying in wide circles. She felt sand under her feet. A gray sea slapped against the rocky shore.

"Look, Will," she said. "Aren't those houses?"

Will shaded his eyes against the afternoon sunlight and looked down the beach. "Maybe they're sheds or boat houses. I don't see any windows, but there are some more carved poles."

Across the water Amanda could see woods and a mountain. "This must be a bay. What a beautiful place!"

The mountain was very different from the rolling green mountains where Amanda and Will had gone to camp last summer.

This mountain poked a rocky point out of a thick forest of tall, dark green trees. Soft clouds drifted around it.

A cool breeze was blowing from the water.

"I don't know where we are," Will said, "but I like it here. It's just as cool as it was in the museum."

Along the shore the trees were bright green and smaller than the forest trees.

Amanda pointed at a patch of scraggly bushes. "Will, I think those are raspberries!"

"What are we waiting for?" Will raced across the sand. Amanda ran after him.

Will stared at the berries on the bushes. "They're bigger than raspberries, and they're orange. I wonder if they're good to eat." He reached out to pick one.

Before Will could touch the berry, the two children heard a voice yell, "Stop!"

3

"YOU'D better not touch those berries!" A boy wearing only a shirt of woven fiber stepped from behind a willow tree.

"Oh!" Amanda tried not to stare at him. "Will they poison us?"

The boy seemed to be older than Will,

but not quite as old as Amanda. He looked at them with bright, dark eyes. Then he laughed. "Where have you been all your lives? Don't you know you can't pick berries from somebody else's patch?"

"We didn't know anybody owned this land," Will said.

"This berry patch belongs to the family of our neighbor, Crooked Toe Eagle. I don't want him to think I've been taking his berries. He's so greedy he'd probably claim the right to take fish from our stream." The boy was looking at Will and Amanda's clothes now. "You're strangers. What are your names?"

"I'm Amanda," she told him. "And this is my brother, Will."

The boy pushed a strand of straight black hair out of his eyes. "I've never heard those names before. What do they mean?"

"Mom said my name is short for William

and means 'bold defender,' and Mandy's name means 'lovable'—which she isn't always." Will grinned.

"What's your name?" Amanda asked.

"Fox-of-the-Water," the boy said.

"Why did your parents give you such a name?" Will wanted to know.

"It was my mother's grandfather's name. He died before I was born," Fox-of-the-Water told them.

"Mandy's named after Mom's grandmother," Will said. "But why did your great-grandfather have a name like that?"

"He was named after an uncle who died before he was born. It's an old family name. Long ago someone was saved from drowning by one of the fox people. There's a song about it that we sometimes sing."

Fox-of-the-Water looked at the sun. "It's getting late," he said. "I ought to be working now. If you want berries, come and help me pick our salmon berries. They're just as good as these of old Crooked Toe Eagle." He went back to the willow tree.

"Mandy," Will whispered, "he's just like the picture of an Indian I saw in my social studies book."

Amanda nodded. "I know the picture you mean. It's in the chapter on totem poles."

The two children stared at each other. Suddenly Amanda remembered. "The book said this was how the Totem Pole Indians looked long ago!"

Neither Will nor Amanda spoke, but now they both knew what had happened.

The black mirror in the museum had taken them into the past!

4

FOX-of-the-Water pulled a large basket from behind the willow tree. "My mother told me to fill this with berries."

Will and Amanda went over to look at the basket.

"Wow! Where are you going to find enough berries to fill anything this size?" Will wanted to know. "And how will you ever pick them all?"

"We'd better get started. Where's your berry patch?" Amanda asked.

"Follow me." The Indian boy tied the basket on his back. He started walking swiftly along the stony beach.

Amanda and Will came after him. They were wearing sneakers, but they had a hard time keeping up with the barefoot Indian.

The three children came to a big cedar log lying on the beach. Someone must have been cutting into it. Patches of the bark had been peeled off, and bits of wood were scattered around.

Fox-of-the-Water took off the basket. He walked slowly around the log and picked up three short, wide pieces of wood. Then he sat down on a rock and used the bone knife hanging around his neck to split one end of each piece into five strips.

"I thought you were in a hurry to get the berries picked, Fox-of-the-Water," Will said. "Why are you wasting time whittling?"

Fox-of-the-Water didn't answer. Instead he went over to the fallen log and began to peel off a long piece of the soft inner bark.

Amanda saw that he was making something. "Fox-of-the-Water," she said, "what can I do to help?"

The Indian boy smiled. "Hold this while I work. Roll it up as I cut it away from the tree." He handed her the end of the piece of bark. "Be careful not to tear it." He went back to pulling the bark from the log.

When Fox-of-the-Water had a long piece of bark, he cut it off. Amanda rolled it up.

Will helped Amanda roll the bark back and forth to make it stronger. The Indian boy cut the bark into three narrow strings and used them to bind the unsplit end of each piece of wood to hold it together.

After that Fox-of-the-Water stuck bits of wood between the strips to spread them apart like the fingers of a hand. He started to sharpen the points.

"Mandy," Will whispered, "what do you think he's going to do with those things?"

5

FOX-of-the-Water dropped one of the spiky wooden things he had made into his basket and handed the other two to Amanda and Will.

"Thank you." Amanda stared at the five sharp points. "What do you use it for?"

"Don't you know a berry picker when you see one?" The Indian boy put the basket on his back and began trotting down the beach again.

Will and Amanda raced after him. They went around a curve of the shore and came to a little stream that trickled out of a tangle of broken bushes and flowed across the sand into the bay.

Fox-of-the-Water stepped into the shallow stream and started wading into the center of the clump of bushes.

Amanda and Will pulled off their sneakers and socks, hung them around their necks, and followed the young Indian.

He stepped out of the stream at a place where the bushes were loaded with the same kind of big orange raspberries that Will and Amanda had seen earlier.

"I wonder why these bushes have so many berries on them," Will said. "I didn't see any a minute ago."

"Aunt Snow Rainbow and my cousins were picking here yesterday," Fox-of-the-Water told him. "They left these bushes for me." He took a mat of woven bark out of the basket and unrolled it on the ground. Then he began to rip branches off the bushes and pile them onto the mat.

"I thought you were going to pick the berries," Amanda said.

"First I have to lay all the branches with berries on this mat," the Indian boy told her. "If you're hungry, eat a few now. Then you can help me."

Will and Amanda each tasted a berry.

"Yum," Amanda said. She started pulling off branches and putting them on the mat.

Will was stacking branches now, too. Now and then he pulled off a berry to eat it. "Not bad. I was afraid they'd taste like fish. They must be called salmon berries because of the color."

Amanda was afraid it would get dark before they finished. She set to work to strip the bushes clean of branches.

When every branch with berries was on the mat, Fox-of-the-Water showed Will and Amanda how to whip the branches one at a time with their berry pickers. This knocked the berries onto the mat.

When the mat was covered, the three children picked it up and poured the berries into the basket.

"Now I have to go home," the Indian boy told them. "Where are you going?"

Amanda thought for a moment. Then she said, "Fox-of-the-Water, we don't *know* where we're going."

"We don't even know where we *are*," Will told him.

6

FOX-of-the-Water looked hard at the two children. "Did someone bring you here against your will?"

"We didn't ask to come here, if that's what you mean," Amanda told him.

"What's more," Will put in, "we don't know how we got here."

"Oh!" the Indian boy said in a low voice. "You're *lost!*" He looked as if he thought this was even worse than either Will or Amanda thought it was.

Fox-of-the-Water bit his lip as if to keep from crying.

Amanda put her arm around his shoulders to comfort him. "We'll be all right, Fox-of-the-Water."

"I can tell that you and your brother don't know how to take care of yourselves

in my country," the Indian boy told her.
"You don't even know how to pick berries.

"I could take you to my uncle's house,"
he said. "I live there with my mother
and father. It's a big house. There's
plenty of room."

Still, Fox-of-the-Water looked worried.
"I never asked you what clan you belong
to," he said.

"Clan? What's that?" Will asked.

The Indian stared at him. "Don't your people set up poles?"

"Flagpoles," Will told him. "Dad put one in front of our porch. Next to the school there's a big tall one."

"Well," Fox-of-the-Water said, "what creature is carved on top of the poles?"

"Creature?" Will looked puzzled.

Amanda interrupted. "The only creature you ever see on a flagpole where we live is an eagle."

"An eagle?" Fox-of-the-Water said, as if he couldn't believe his ears.

"Yes," Will agreed. "Never anything but an eagle!"

The young Indian smiled. "Then everything is all right. My family are Eagles." He put the basket on his back. "Come along."

Fox-of-the-Water stepped into the little stream and started wading through the broken berry bushes.

Will and Amanda followed him. When they came to the beach, they put on their socks and sneakers.

The Indian didn't walk so fast now.

"We'd better take turns carrying the basket," Amanda said.

Will helped her lift it off the Indian boy's back and slip her arms through the straps. Amanda carried the basket to the fallen cedar log. Then Will took his turn.

Soon they could see the row of houses along the shore. The first one they came to was very small. Someone was standing in the doorway.

Fox-of-the-Water whispered, "Don't stare at the saya-gay. He might put a spell on you!"

7

A SMALL man with a long gray beard and long gray hair worn in a big knot on top of his head stepped out of the little house. "You are late coming home, Fox-of-the-Water. You should not worry Sunset Moon this way."

Fox-of-the-Water looked at the ground. "I'm sorry, Bright Star," he said. "I didn't mean to worry my mother."

Will put the heavy basket on the ground.

The old man bent over it. "Salmon berries! My favorite!" He went into his hut and came out with a wooden bowl.

Fox-of-the-Water quickly filled the bowl with berries. "I want you to meet my clansfolk, Mandy and Will."

Bright Star looked at the T-shirts and blue jeans and sneakers that the two children were wearing. He was dressed in a soft leather shirt and pants.

Will and Amanda tried hard not to stare at him, but the old man had the longest fingernails they had ever seen. He wore a necklace of bone-and-copper beads and what Will thought must have been bear teeth. The strangest thing of all was the long, thin bone through his nose.

Bright Star looked first into Amanda's eyes and then into Will's. He passed his hand across his eyes. "You two have seen

things I do not understand, but you are good at heart."

He turned to the Indian boy. "You are right to make friends with these young people. You have more sense than I thought, Fox-of-the-Water. Now, go home. Sunset Moon is afraid you have had the bad luck to meet some land-otter people!"

"Thank you, Bright Star." Fox-of-the-Water picked up the basket and walked as fast as he could. Will and Amanda marched alongside.

"Who was that, Fox-of-the-Water?" Amanda asked.

"The saya-gay of our village. He heals the sick and tells us how to stay friends with the salmon people and the bear people and others. The saya-gay is very wise, but you must be careful not to annoy him. He has powerful charms that he could use against you."

"Sounds like a witch doctor," Will whispered in his sister's ear.

"Sh-sh!" Amanda changed the subject. "Who are the land-otter people?" she asked the Indian boy.

"They're the spirits of the land otters when they want to look like people," Fox-of-the-Water told her. "We have to stay clear of them. They're very tricky. They hate us and are always ready to harm us."

"Have you ever seen them?" Will wanted to know.

"No, but my mother has a friend whose grandmother met one in the woods early one morning. After that she couldn't speak." Fox-of-the-Water looked around.

The sky was getting darker. A chill wind blew from the bay. The young Indian began to walk faster.

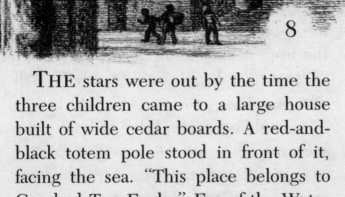

8

THE stars were out by the time the three children came to a large house built of wide cedar boards. A red-and-black totem pole stood in front of it, facing the sea. "This place belongs to Crooked Toe Eagle," Fox-of-the-Water said.

The next house was even bigger. Amanda saw that there was an eagle carved on the top of the painted totem pole at the front of the house. "This must be where you live, Fox-of-the-Water."

The Indian smiled. "Yes," he said. "Come inside. It is the house of my uncle, Mountain Echo."

Will started to walk to a door in the side of the house. Fox-of-the-Water grabbed his arm. "Don't go in there!" he ordered. "That's only for slaves. Follow me." The Indian boy walked around to the front of the totem pole.

"Did you hear that, Mandy?" Will whispered.

Amanda nodded. "I don't like it," she said in a low voice.

Fox-of-the-Water turned to look back at them. "What's keeping you two? I want you to meet my family. Come along!" He carried the basket of berries through an archway cut into the pole.

Will looked at Amanda. She kept her chin high and stood as tall and straight as she could. Then she walked through the round doorway into the house. Will came after her.

They stepped down into a big room. There were three cooking fires, each with a group of people sitting on the ground near it. Another fire burned in the corner of the room where the roof was highest. There was a smoke hole over this fire.

A woman in a shirt and skirt of woven bark ran across the room. "Fox-of-the-Water, where have you been? You're supposed to be home before dark!"

Fox-of-the-Water took the basket off his back and held it out. He grinned. "Remember, Sunset Moon, you told me I had to pick all the berries Aunt Snow Rainbow left."

His mother looked into the basket. "I didn't think you could do it. I was angry with you for going fishing instead of helping your cousins pick berries this morning." Sunset Moon looked up and saw Amanda and Will. For a moment she just stared at them.

Amanda thought she looked scared.

"It's all right." Fox-of-the-Water put the basket down. "These are my friends, Mandy and Will. They're Eagles, and they helped me pick the berries."

Sunset Moon laughed. "Now I know how you did it!" She smiled at Will and Amanda. "Thank you and welcome."

A tall man with a red-and-black tattoo on his chest walked over. "This is my father, Brave Warrior," Fox-of-the-Water told them.

"We are glad to have you with us," Brave Warrior said. "You must be hungry. Come and have some supper."

Amanda and Will followed him to a cooking fire on the other side of the big room.

9

SUPPER was the strangest meal either Amanda or Will had ever eaten, but they were so hungry that it tasted wonderful.

Sunset Moon handed each of them a wooden bowl and bone spoon. She used a dipper made of shell to fill the bowls with chunks of stewed fish from one square wooden box and stewed roots from another.

A woman was picking hot stones from the fire with two long, flat sticks. She dropped the stones into the boxes to keep the stew warm.

The three children sat on the ground to eat. Fox-of-the-Water showed Will and Amanda how to dip the fish and the roots into a bowl of sweet oil.

Sunset Moon had put the big basket of salmon berries down beside them. Fox-of-the-Water dipped the berries into the oil, too. Amanda tried this and decided to eat her berries plain. Will said he liked his dipped in oil, but Amanda thought he was only pretending to dunk.

Both Will and Amanda saw that the people here did not wear much clothing.

Nobody spoke to the woman who was putting the hot stones into the boxes.

There were other people in the room who were busy working. They were

spoken to only when something needed to be done.

"Fox-of-the-Water," Amanda whispered, "what's the name of the lady over there by the fire?"

"I don't know," he said. "She's only a slave."

Will heard this. "She has to use the side door! Is she being punished for something, Fox-of-the-Water?"

The young Indian thought for a minute. "She made the mistake of letting herself be captured."

"I don't understand," Amanda told him.

"When we need help with our work," Fox-of-the-Water said, "the men make a raid on another village to capture slaves. Sometimes our men are hurt or killed. When things go well, they bring back slaves. Of course, if a captive is a member of one of the clans in our village, we have to pay for any damage and return the captive."

Now Will and Amanda knew why Fox-of-the-Water was so happy to think that they belonged to the Eagle clan. He didn't want them to be made slaves!

Fox-of-the-Water pointed to the other cooking fires. "Those belong to the families of my aunts and cousins. The one under the smoke hole is the household fire. We never let that go out. In winter it's much bigger."

Will showed Amanda rows of fish hanging from racks high over the fires.

"I guess that's how they smoke the fish," she said.

Suddenly Fox-of-the-Water jumped to his feet. "Stand up!" he whispered. "My uncle, Mountain Echo, is coming."

10

AMANDA saw an Indian wearing copper rings on his arms and legs coming toward them. There were tattoos on the backs of his hands and on his chest.

Sunset Moon and Brave Warrior left their places near the cooking fire and went to greet the owner of the house. They walked with him to where the three children were standing.

"Good evening, Fox-of-the-Water," his uncle said.

"Good evening, Mountain Echo," the Indian boy answered. "I want you to meet my friends, Mandy and Will. They are Eagles from a strange country."

"Thank you for letting us come to your house," Amanda said.

"We've never seen anything like it," Will told him.

Mountain Echo smiled. He had a strong but gentle face. "I believe you." He touched Will's T-shirt. "And I have never seen clothes like yours." He looked at Will and then at Amanda. "You are welcome to stay with us." He turned to Sunset Moon. "Sister, our guests will need sleeping mats and blankets. If you do not have enough, there are some stored under my sleeping platform."

Mountain Echo stroked the top of Fox-of-the-Water's head. He smiled again and walked back to the rear of the house.

The people in the room had finished eating. They all took their bowls and spoons outside and scrubbed them with sand from the beach. Fox-of-the-Water showed Amanda and Will where his family's dishes were stored under a raised platform that ran along the inside wall of the house.

The walls were hung with mats made

of rushes stitched together with cattail fiber. Finer mats of soft inner cedar bark divided the big room into sections for each family.

Sunset Moon gave Amanda and Will each a sleeping mat and a blanket of some sort of wool.

Will spread his sleeping mat on the wooden platform next to where Fox-of-the-Water was already asleep. Amanda put her mat beside his.

Will lay down and rolled himself up in his blanket. "Mandy," he whispered, "this isn't bad at all."

The mats were made of two layers of rushes crowded together so tightly that they were bouncy.

Amanda took off her sneakers and curled up under the blanket. Everybody else in the big room seemed to be asleep now, even her brother. The fires were still burning. They were very low, but they cast strange flickering shadows everywhere in the big room.

Amanda wondered if this were all a dream and she would wake up tomorrow in her own bed in Brooklyn. She was much too tired to think about it, and in half a minute she was fast asleep.

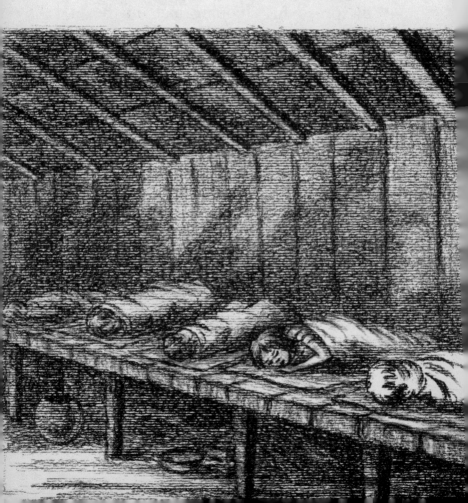

11

AMANDA woke to the sound of singing. She opened her eyes. At first she didn't know where she was. It seemed to be a large, dimly lit room.

Then Amanda remembered what had happened yesterday. She sat up. The fires still burned with a dull red glow, but now a little daylight was shining through the smoke hole in the roof.

Amanda looked around for her brother. She couldn't see him anywhere. Her heart started to pound, but she took a deep breath and tried to pretend she wasn't scared.

She put on her sneakers and rolled up her blanket in her sleeping mat. All the other mats were stored out of sight under the platform. Amanda put her bedding there, too.

The singing seemed to be coming from outdoors. Amanda crossed the room to the big arched doorway. She had to step up to go out into the morning sunshine.

The bay was crowded with boats. They were different sizes, but they were all hollowed out of cedar logs. The people in the boats were singing. And all the other people of the village were standing barefoot on the beach and singing, too. The sky was blue, and the sea was sparkling. Most of the children had no clothes on now. They were dripping wet and must have been swimming.

Will was next to Fox-of-the-Water, listening to the words of the song. It was about a time long ago when animals and people and spirits could change places. Almost everybody seemed to know the words and was singing loudly. They all looked as if they were having a wonderful time.

When the song ended, Amanda went to join the two boys. "Why didn't you wake me?"

"Fox-of-the-Water was in a rush to join in the singing," Will said. "And I wanted to see what was going on."

Amanda didn't want to admit how frightened she had been. She listened as the singers sang three more songs. Then some of them paddled away in their dugout canoes. Others went off to work or to eat.

There were cooking fires burning outdoors now. Will and Amanda followed Fox-of-the-Water to where Sunset Moon was pouring the salmon berries from the berry basket into a wooden box in which water was boiling. The slave woman was adding more hot stones to the water.

Fox-of-the-Water handed bowls and spoons to Amanda and Will. "Take what you want from those." He pointed to more wooden boxes near the fire.

The food was a lot like what they had eaten the night before, but it was fresh and good-tasting. And it was fun to eat breakfast in the open air.

When they had finished eating, Sunset Moon handed each of the three children a round basket. She smiled at Amanda. "Please don't let Fox-of-the-Water go fishing until he brings me fresh water."

12

FOX-of-the-Water led the way back along the beach where they had walked the day before.

"What will we put the water in?" Will asked him.

The Indian waved the basket he was carrying. "In these, of course."

"I never knew baskets could hold water," Amanda said.

"They're easier to carry than wooden boxes," Fox-of-the-Water told her.

The children came to the little house where the saya-gay lived. Bright Star was sitting on the wooden platform in front of his house. He was busy making something and didn't seem to notice them. Fox-of-the-Water put his finger to his lips and tiptoed around the house to reach a path into the woods.

The path led through a grove of trees with tiny green crab apples on them. In sunny spots between the trees Amanda saw patches of big purple clover.

They walked until they came to a line of willow trees growing on the bank of a creek. Fox-of-the-Water leaned over to fill his basket with water. Amanda and Will filled theirs, too.

The three children picked up the water baskets and were about to turn around and go back the way they had come. They looked up and saw something leaning over the creek.

It was a mother bear! And beside her were two little cubs.

The children stayed as still as they could, hoping the bears had not seen them.

The mother bear was staring down into the creek. The three children saw her reach into the water. A second later the bear had a big fish in her long, sharp claws. She threw it onto the bank and turned around to eat it. Both the two little bears tried to get a bite of the fish at the same time. Their mother growled and pushed them away.

When she had eaten all that she wanted, the big bear turned away from the fish and left it for her cubs to finish. She sniffed the air.

At once all the hair on the bear's back stood on end. She looked around and caught sight of the children. Her little eyes seemed to glow red.

Keeping between her cubs and the children, the bear began to move closer.

None of the children wanted to run away and leave the others behind.

Amanda swung her water basket and splashed the bear in the face. This only made the bear angrier. She stood up on her hind legs and made a dive for Amanda.

At this moment there was a loud rattling noise. Amanda was so startled that she slipped on a patch of damp moss and fell in front of the bear.

13

AT any moment Amanda expected to feel the sharp claws or the teeth of the bear. Instead she heard that rattling noise and the sound of laughter.

She looked up to see the black bear running into the woods after her frightened cubs. A strange creature with the head of a fish was chasing the bears. The fish creature was shaking a rattle and laughing at the same time.

Amanda stood up. She saw her brother

and the Indian boy standing side by side with their mouths open. Amanda thought they looked like fish, too. She began to laugh and couldn't stop.

Fox-of-the-Water whispered, "Be careful! Nobody laughs at the saya-gay!"

The bear and her cubs went crashing through the underbrush toward the deeper woods away from the shore. Then the witch doctor turned around and came back to the children.

He took off the carved wooden mask he was wearing. "I just finished making this for the Welcome Salmon Day, and I wanted to show it to somebody. It's lucky that I came here." He looked at the sky. "The Power of the Shining Heavens must be watching over you."

"Thank you for chasing away the bear, Bright Star." Amanda looked at the mask. She saw that the fish's eyes were made of pearly shell and the mask was painted black and red. She smiled at the saya-gay. "It's a wonderful fish, Bright Star. I'm sure the salmon will like it."

Bright Star smiled back at her. In spite of the bone he wore in his nose, Amanda thought he had a nice face. "That sort of bear is usually timid," the witch doctor told her. "This one was trying to protect her babies. And she knew that you were afraid of her. If she had been one of those fierce bears, I couldn't have scared her away so easily." He turned to the boys. "I think Sunset Moon must have asked you to fetch water. She won't like to be kept waiting."

"You saved Mandy's life, Bright Star. Thank you." Will held out his hand.

The witch doctor held the fish mask and the rattle with one hand and took hold of Will's hand with the other. "You do not know how happy this has made me," the witch doctor said.

Fox-of-the-Water bowed. "My family is in your debt, Bright Star."

"It is an honor, Fox-of-the-Water." The saya-gay bowed. "I must return to my work." He walked back toward his house.

Amanda picked up her water basket and filled it from the creek.

"You were both very brave," Fox-of-the-Water said.

"We weren't any braver than you," Amanda reminded him. "Bright Star was the brave one."

"Bright Star has magic power over animals — and over people, too," the young Indian told them. "I would not have the courage to laugh or even smile at him. Nor would anyone here. And I would never be brave enough to touch his hand the way you do!"

14

THE three children walked as fast as they could with the heavy baskets of water. Sunset Moon was waiting for them beside her outdoor cooking fire.

The salmon berries had been stewed to a mush and were now spread out on mats to dry in the sun.

Sunset Moon put the baskets of water in a shady place near the wall of the house. She handed Fox-of-the-Water a strange basket that looked like a long tube with a funnel at one end.

"You take one end and let Will hold

the other," Sunset Moon said. "Mandy, do you think you can carry the burden basket?"

"Yes," Mandy said, wondering what the burden basket was like.

Sunset Moon strapped a basket with a flat bottom to Mandy's back. "Good fishing!" She went back to her work by the fire.

"Why didn't you tell your mother about the bear?" Amanda asked the Indian boy.

"I'm supposed to watch out for bears. I didn't want to be punished." Fox-of-the-Water led the way along the beach. He held the wide end of the long, skinny basket. Will had the narrow end. Amanda came after with the burden basket on her back.

When they came near the saya-gay's house, they saw the witch doctor talking to an old woman. He was holding a box of carved and polished black stone.

Bright Star scooped out three handfuls of dried plants from his stone box and dropped them into a wooden bowl the woman had in her hand. "Stir these into a very little water and put them on your aches. They will make your skin feel hot, but the pain will go. Save these herbs and use them whenever you need them."

The woman bowed low and went away, carrying her bowl.

The saya-gay walked over to the children.

"Where did you get the beautiful box?" Mandy asked.

Bright Star smiled. "I made it. I'm always looking for pieces of this kind of rock. If you find any, let me know." He looked at the long, skinny basket the boys were carrying. "Where are you going to fish?"

"In the little stream Mountain Echo gave to Brave Warrior last winter," Fox-of-the-Water told him.

"I wish you luck." The medicine man went back to his house.

Fox-of-the-Water walked faster. Will had to hurry to keep up. Amanda marched after them.

15

The Indian boy turned away from the beach and went into the woods. Amanda couldn't see a path, but he seemed to know where he was going. The farther they went from the shore, the deeper the woods became. Amanda looked hard at every shadow. She didn't want to meet another bear.

The trees were different from the ones at the shore. They were much taller, and they were evergreens. Thick moss made a carpet on the ground and covered the branches overhead.

Fox-of-the-Water walked slowly. He seemed to be listening.

Amanda was beginning to think they were lost when she heard the splash and gurgle of a stream.

"Here we are!" Fox-of-the-Water said.

The dark branches of the trees did not meet above the little stream. The blue sky could be seen here, and the rippling water sparkled in the sun.

Fox-of-the-Water stepped into the stream.

Will put down his end of the long, skinny basket and took off his socks and sneakers. Amanda slipped out of the straps of the burden basket and set it down. By the time her feet were bare, both boys were in the stream with the basket tube.

Amanda waded into the cool water and went to help them.

Fox-of-the-Water placed the wide end of the basket downstream. He showed Will and Amanda how to put sticks and underbrush across the stream on either side of the long tube so the fish could not swim upstream, except through the tube.

The Indian Boy climbed out of the water and began to walk along the bank. Amanda and Will went after him.

The stream became wider and deeper. Fox-of-the-Water cut three leafy branches from a bush. He gave one to Amanda and one to Will. With the third he started to whip the water of the stream.

"What are you doing?" Will asked.

"Trying to scare the fish, of course,"
Fox-of-the-Water told him.

Will and Amanda rolled their jean legs
high over their knees and waded into
the water, beating it with the leafy
branches. They followed Fox-of-the-
Water back up the stream to where they
had left the fish trap.

The Indian boy leaned over the long
tube and peeked through the basketwork.
He picked up the wide funnel end and
started to drag the heavy fish trap to the
shore of the stream. Amanda and Will
helped him lift it onto the mossy bank,

where Amanda had left the burden basket.

Now Will looked into the trap. "Wow!"

Fox-of-the-Water placed the wide end of the tube in the burden basket and held it steady while Amanda and Will lifted the narrow end into the air.

The tube was full of fish. There was no room in it for them to turn around and swim out. The children dumped them out, tail-first, into the flat-bottomed basket.

Amanda tried to pick it up. "We won't be able to carry all these. Let's put the little ones back."

"Not these." Fox-of-the-Water held up a slender, silvery fish. "Sunset Moon uses them to make oil." He chose all the fish he wanted to keep. Will and Amanda let the others go free in the stream.

16

"I'M hungry," Fox-of-the-Water said.

"So am I," Amanda told him.

"Me, too." Will looked around. "I see blueberries over there. Are we allowed to eat them?"

"I don't know if Mountain Echo gave the berry patch to Brave Warrior along with the stream," Fox-of-the-Water said, "but neither of them would mind if we ate some with our meal. It would be different if we picked all of them. We can eat a few while the fish is cooking."

The Indian boy pulled a handful of dried cedar bark out of a leather bag that hung at his waist. He found a hardwood stick.

Amanda and Will watched him twirl the stick back and forth like a drill in the soft, woolly bark.

"Get some firewood ready," he said. He went on twirling.

By the time they had gathered a pile of dry twigs and sticks of all sizes, a tiny flame was flickering in the dry cedar bark. The children added wood little by little until they had a cooking fire.

Fox-of-the-Water used his bone knife to clean a large fish. He set it close to the fire. The fish was held upright in a split stick tied together at the top with a piece of cedar bark.

When the fish was cooked on one side,

Amanda turned the stick so that the other side faced the heat.

All three children took turns watching to make sure the fish did not burn. In between watching, they nibbled blueberries off the bush.

Amanda picked three very large leaves from a plant growing near the stream. "We can use these for plates."

As soon as the fish was cooked, Fox-of-the-Water cut thick slices off it. They all ate with their fingers. Amanda and Will had never known that fish could taste so good. Everybody had second and third helpings.

After the meal, Will and Amanda put their sneakers on. Will kicked dirt onto the fire and stamped on it. Amanda and Fox-of-the-Water cupped their hands and brought water from the stream to soak the ground.

The burden basket was heavy with

fish now. The three children tried taking turns at first. Then they looped the straps so that they could all get a grip on the basket. They walked back through the dark woods, stopping now and then to put down the basket and rest.

After what seemed an age, the trees became smaller and brighter green. Still the children walked and walked. They were hot and tired when at last they came out onto the sunny beach. They set the basket down in the shadow of a rock.

"I'm going for a swim!" Fox-of-the-Water took the knife from around his neck, the leather bag from his waist, slipped out of his shirt, and put everything under a stone. He raced across the sand and splashed into the little foaming waves. "Come on in. The water's fine!"

17

WILL and Amanda took off their sneakers. They ran to the water and jumped in.

Fox-of-the-Water was swimming dog-paddle style. After a while he stopped and watched Will and Amanda. They had both learned to swim at the Y.

"I wish I could swim like that," the Indian boy said. "You go so much faster than I do."

"We could teach you how," Amanda told him.

The Indian boy looked at the sun. "Maybe tomorrow," he said. "We'd better get home with those fish."

The tide had gone out since they started swimming. The wet sand was covered with oysters.

"If we didn't have such a heavy load in the basket, we could take these back to Sunset Moon," Fox-of-the-Water said. "She loves oysters."

Amanda saw a black stone sticking up under a pile of shells. "That looks like the same kind of stone Bright Star used for his beautiful box!"

"That stone is good for making arrowheads," Fox-of-the-Water said. "The saya-gay might give me the leftover chips. I need some new arrows." He started to dig the stone out of the sand.

"If we don't get it now, the sea may take it back again."

Will and Amanda helped him raise the stone. It was nearly two feet long and almost as wide, but it was thin and flat like a piece of slate. The three children carried the stone above the high-water mark on the beach and hid it under a bush. Amanda broke a twig off the bush.

Will was shivering now.

"We're taught to run up and down the beach after a swim until we're warm." Fox-of-the-Water started running.

Will and Amanda decided to run, too.

As soon as they were warm again, the children picked up the basket of fish and carried it back along the beach.

The saya-gay was sitting on the platform in front of his house, making something out of feathers. He came over to look into the basket. "Ah!" He lifted out a shining fish. "This will do for my supper."

18

AMANDA thought Bright Star was very rude. He never said "please" or "thank you" and just took what he wanted. She waited for Fox-of-the-Water to tell the saya-gay about the black stone. The Indian boy didn't say a word. He always seemed to be frightened of the witch doctor.

Still, there was something about the little man that had made Amanda like him even before he had saved her from the bear.

"Bright Star," she said, "we found a black rock like the one you used for your box."

The saya-gay was so excited that he almost dropped the fish he was holding by the tail. "Where did you see this rock, Mandy? I'd like to get it before anyone else finds it." He put the fish into a basket of water near the door of his house.

"It was in the wet sand at low tide," Will told him. "We dug it out and hid it under a bush."

Bright Star went into his house and came out with a mat rolled up under his arm. "Mandy," he said, "would you please show me where to find the rock?"

"First I have to help the boys carry these fish to Sunset Moon," Mandy told him.

"We don't need help, Mandy!" Fox-of-the-Water said.

"Let me fix those straps." Bright Star

looped the burden straps to make a double harness. The boys were side by side now, with the basket on their backs. They trotted off like a pair of ponies.

"Come on, Mandy." The saya-gay carried his rolled-up mat over one shoulder and walked beside Amanda. They talked as they went along.

"Why are you so polite and friendly to Will and me and so mean to Fox-of-the-Water?" Amanda asked. "He's scared of you."

It was a little while before Bright Star answered. "Something tells me you're very different, and I can talk to you. I have to keep all these people afraid of me or I can't help them. If they thought I was just like them, they wouldn't believe in me. It's lonely. I haven't talked to anybody like this since I was thirteen years old. That's when I knew I was going to be a saya-gay."

"Why did you become one?" Amanda wanted to know.

"My uncle was a saya-gay, and my family always thought I should be one someday, too. Saya-gays are born different from other people. I had dreams about things that would happen and knew what people were thinking. When I was thirteen, I had a vision of a bright light coming from the sky. That was a sign that I was meant to be a saya-gay.

"I had to let my hair and nails grow, and this bone was put through my nose. The tribe sent me into the woods to make friends with the animals. No one else has been my friend until you and your brother came along.

"I have the strangest dreams about you. You don't belong in this time or place. Tell me how you came here."

19

Amanda told Bright Star all about Brooklyn and the museum and how she and Will had looked into the black mirror and been taken back in time.

The saya-gay kept stopping her to ask questions. Amanda told him that the museum was a very big house built of stone where old, old things were kept. He understood that the totem poles there were so old that all the paint was gone, and the wood was worn and broken, but he didn't know what a mirror was. When they came to a little tidewater pool on the beach, Amanda leaned over to look into it. She saw herself reflected

in the still water. "A mirror is like this, Bright Star. You can see yourself in it, only it isn't water. A mirror is flat and hard and shiny."

Amanda went on to tell how she and Will had looked into the magic mirror and what had happened afterward. "This is a wonderful place to be," she told the saya-gay, "but I keep worrying about how we'll get home. Our mother and father must think something terrible has happened to us."

Bright Star tugged at his scraggly beard. "Mandy, stop worrying! That never does any good." He smiled at her. "Tell yourself that everything will be all right."

Amanda felt better at once. "Look, Bright Star, here's the bush where we hid your rock!" She leaned over and pushed back the branches that covered it.

The saya-gay leaned over to touch the black rock. "How did you know which bush it was under, Mandy? They look so much alike I was afraid you wouldn't find it."

Mandy pulled a green twig out of her jeans pocket and showed him where she'd taken it off the bush. "I kept it to match with the bush—just in case another bush had a broken branch."

Bright Star unrolled the mat he was carrying and lifted the rock onto it. Then he took hold of one corner of the mat, and Amanda grabbed another. Together they started dragging the mat across the sand.

Long before they reached the saya-gay's house they saw Will and Fox-of-the-Water running to meet them.

Now the boys helped Amanda pull the mat. Bright Star followed behind, making sure that the rock was safely moved.

"Sunset Moon wants all of us in the house before dark," Fox-of-the-Water said. "She told me to warn you and Will not to drink from the streams or wade in the water once the sun goes down."

"Why not?" Will asked.

"The land otters bewitch the streams and lakes after sunset," the Indian boy told them. He lowered his voice to a whisper. "Of course, Bright Star is safe. *He* has a powerful charm to protect him from the otters."

20

THE saya-gay said good-bye to the children and took the black rock into his little house.

Fox-of-the-Water began to run. Will and Amanda chased after him. As they came near the line of houses, they heard singing. The people of the village were ending the day as they had begun it, standing on the beach to sing. The boats were all pulled up onto the beach.

When the songs were done, they all went into their houses. Most of those in Mountain Echo's house had already eaten supper, but there was still plenty of food in the wooden boxes by the fire. It didn't seem to annoy anyone that the children were late. People ate whenever they were hungry.

While they were eating, Amanda noticed that a row of drums was being set up on the big platform at the rear of the house. "What's happening over there, Fox-of-the-Water?"

"Someone in Aunt Snow Rainbow's family must be sick," Fox-of-the-Water told her. "They're getting ready for the saya-gay. Come and watch."

Will and Amanda gobbled down the rest of the food in their wooden bowls. They ran outside to clean the bowls before putting them away.

Mountain Echo had gone to fetch the saya-gay. While they were waiting for him to arrive, Snow Rainbow laid a boy about five years old on a sleeping mat in the middle of the platform. A line of people sat down behind the drums.

Then Bright Star walked into the house. Mountain Echo came after him. The big room was very quiet.

The saya-gay set down a large basket on the platform. He took out a cord decorated with feathers and stretched it around the little boy.

"That's to protect him," Fox-of-the-Water whispered.

Bright Star took the mask of an old woman's spirit from his basket. He danced back and forth while the drums beat softly. The saya-gay changed into the mask of a bear spirit, then to an old man's spirit. Next he was a spirit living in the clouds.

Each time the saya-gay changed masks, the drums beat a little louder and Bright Star danced faster. When at last he put on a red mask with a wolf on top and three otters on each side, the little man was dancing like a whirlwind.

Suddenly he stopped and leaned over the sick child. Bright Star took off his mask. He put his mouth first on the boy's chest, then on his throat.

"He's sucking out the sickness," Fox-of-the-Water said.

The saya-gay blew a long breath toward the smoke hole in the roof.

The people in the room smiled at each other. Amanda and Will could see they all believed Bright Star had blown the sickness away.

Snow Rainbow held out a little bowl shaped like a boat. The saya-gay put three handfuls of herbs into it. "Mix these with a little water and put it on your son's chest," he told her. "Keep him quiet, and make him drink water. He'll be better in the morning."

FOX-of-the-Water's little cousin was much better the next morning. It was a damp, drizzly day, so he couldn't go out to play, even if his mother had let him.

On cloudy days everybody stayed indoors. Some of the people were making baskets. Sunset Moon set up a big loom and began to weave cedar bark string into a blanket. She taught Amanda to twist duck feathers into strings that were woven across the cloth.

Fox-of-the-Water showed Will his bow and a sealskin case big enough to hold twelve arrows. Together the two boys made a bow for Will out of wood from a yew tree. They wrapped the ends of the stick in wet seaweed and buried it in the warm ground very near the cooking fire. The wood steamed until it was soft enough to be bent easily. A cord was made of the strong sinew from a walrus.

"I've been saving the right kind of sticks to make arrows," Fox-of-the-Water said, "but we have to make arrowheads."

"Do you have feathers for them?" Will asked.

"We don't use feathers on our arrows," the Indian boy told him.

In the afternoon Bright Star came to the big house. He put a little leather bag on the ground between Will and Fox-of-the-Water. "Make good use of these!"

The saya-gay was wearing a pointed basket hat to keep off the rain. He visited the little boy he had cured the night before and then went back to his own house.

Will opened the leather bag and poured twelve pieces of black stone into his hand. "Thanks for telling Bright Star that Fox-of-the-Water wanted these, Mandy."

"I forgot to tell him," Amanda said.

"That's spooky," Will whispered.

"He has second sight," Fox-of-the-Water said. He took one of the pieces of black stone and began to chip at it with a heavy stone pounder.

Amanda tried to tell herself that Bright Star must have thought Fox-of-the-Water needed arrowheads. Everybody seemed to find reasons to be afraid of the saya-gay. But Amanda liked Bright Star. She decided to go and visit him the next day.

The next day wasn't just drizzling. It was raining hard. It rained for three days. Everybody stayed indoors and worked. The saya-gay came to the big house to get food that he took back to his own place. He never stopped to talk to the children.

Then one morning Amanda was awakened by singing. All the people in the village were outdoors again, in their boats or on the beach. The rain had stopped, and the sky was a clear deep blue. Sunlight danced across the water.

Amanda had never seen such a beautiful day.

22

WHEN the singing was over, Mountain Echo stood on the platform in front of his house and raised his arm. The people on the beach all became quiet.

"The Ripe Berry Moon is almost over. The Salmon Moon will soon be here. Today we will do the salmon dance." Mountain Echo put on a mask with two red spots on the forehead, three black marks on the left cheek, and three red marks on the right. He picked up a carved and painted wooden salmon.

Bright Star came out of the big doorway in the totem pole to join Mountain Echo.

The saya-gay was wearing the beautiful fish mask he had made. The two of them walked to the edge of the water.

The people followed them, dancing and singing. Then Bright Star called to the water spirits and begged them to bring back the salmon.

After that the canoes were paddled away, and everybody on shore went about their daily routine.

Amanda and the two boys went to get

something to eat from the wooden boxes by the cooking fire.

"When the salmon return," Fox-of-the-Water said, "we will all go and camp by the rivers while we're catching the fish. It's fun. Instead of living with uncles and aunts and cousins in one big house, each family has its own little shelter of brushwood."

"Will that be soon?" Amanda asked.

"Maybe the day after tomorrow," the Indian boy told her. "It all depends on the salmon."

"You promised to teach me how to use the bow and arrow, Fox-of-the-Water," Will said. "Why don't we do it today?"

Amanda had finished eating. "I don't want to risk getting in the way of your arrows, Will." She stood up. "Make him be careful, Fox-of-the-Water. I'll see you both later."

Amanda walked along the beach toward Bright Star's little house. When she got there she heard a scraping sound coming from inside.

A mat hung over the doorway. Amanda went close to it and called, "Bright Star!"

The scraping stopped. The saya-gay slipped out of the doorway without moving the mat enough to let Amanda see into his house. "Mandy! I thought it was you. Is anything wrong?"

"I just came to visit," Amanda told him. "Will and Fox-of-the-Water are busy with their bows and arrows."

"I know you think I'm rude," the witch doctor said, "but I haven't time for a visit. I'm working on something."

"What is it?" Amanda asked.

"If I tell you, it will break the spell." Bright Star went back into his house.

23

AMANDA felt as if she had been slapped in the face. She bit her lip to keep from crying.

She went back to the Eagle house to help Sunset Moon make cakes of dried berries and pack them away for later use.

When the tide was out, Sunset Moon put a mat on her back. "That's to keep me dry," she said. "Come along. I'll show you how we dig clams."

The Indian woman jabbed the pointed end of a short, flat stick deep into the mud and twirled the other end. At once a great many clams came up out of the wet sand. Sunset Moon bent over at the hips as if she wanted to touch her feet with her face. She quickly reached all around to gather the best clams before the tide returned.

Sunset Moon and Amanda roasted some of the clams over the open fire and shared them with the slave woman. They put the rest into one of the wooden boxes to steam.

When the boys came back from their bow-and-arrow practice, they ate steamed clams and clover roots.

The day became very warm in the afternoon. All three children went swimming in the bay. Both Amanda and Will showed Fox-of-the-Water the strokes they had learned at the Y.

The Indian boy reminded them to get out of the water before sunset. "If you don't," he warned, "you will be forever in the power of the land otters!"

The people in the boats returned before sunset, too. They dragged the heavy canoes up onto the beach as the evening singing began.

Amanda was so tired by the time she

lay down on her mat that she fell asleep at once.

Some time later in the night she woke. The big house was stuffy from the smoldering fires. Amanda got up and walked to the archway in the totem pole to get a breath of fresh air.

She looked across the bay.

A pale moon was rising above the mountain. By its light Amanda saw something moving on the water. It seemed to be a huge canoe, but of course it couldn't be. The people of this tribe would not go out of the house on a cloudy day because they thought bad spirits were around them. They surely would not go out on the water at night!

Suddenly Amanda had a terrible thought. Perhaps the people in the canoe came from a different tribe who were not afraid of the dark. They might be coming to this village to capture slaves!

There was not a moment to lose. Amanda raced back to the fire and grabbed one of the fish that was used to make oil. She held it to the flame. The fish burned like a candle.

"Wake up!" She held the blazing fish high and yelled as loud as she could. "Wake up! A big canoe is coming!"

24

MOUNTAIN Echo was up and dressed in a wooden helmet and armor made of wooden slats before most of the other people were awake. "Go next door, Mandy. Tell Crooked Toe Eagle what you have seen." He turned to Fox-of-the-Water. "You and Will must warn the people in the other houses of the village. Hurry!"

Brave Warrior was in armor now, too. He started handing spears, clubs, and bows and arrows to the rest of the people in the house.

Amanda didn't stop to put on her sneakers. She rushed barefoot to the house next door, holding the burning candle-fish.

The doorway of this house was covered by a mat. Amanda had to push it aside to get into the room. The room was very dark and smelled stale. The people were all asleep, and many of them were snoring.

Amanda yelled, "Wake up!" several times, but everybody went right on sleeping.

She ran over to the platform at the back of the house. Four men and three women and a number of children were sleeping there.

"Wake up!" Amanda screamed. Still nobody did.

She leaned over the oldest man and shined the light from the candle-fish into his face. He put his hand over his eyes.

Amanda reached out and shook his

shoulder. The man opened his eyes and sat up. "Who are you?" he said in a sleepy voice.

"Mountain Echo sent me to warn you that the village is going to be attacked," Amanda told him. "Get ready to defend yourself!"

The man still kept staring stupidly at her.

Amanda left him and shook each of the other men in turn, screaming, "The enemy is coming!" over and over. By this time the women and children were awake. They seemed to think Amanda was the enemy!

She threw down the burning fish, which was getting very short, and ran back to the front door. Amanda pushed aside the mat hanging over it and slipped out into the open air.

She looked around for her brother, but she didn't see him anywhere.

The moon was higher in the sky. Amanda wondered if the people in the other houses were like those in Crooked Toe Eagle's house. They didn't act like Eagles at all. She looked at the top of the totem pole in front of the house. There seemed to be a frog on top, or maybe, Amanda thought, it was a toad. Amanda began to understand why Fox-of-the-Water was so proud to be an Eagle.

25

AMANDA looked out over the water. The giant canoe was much nearer now. She could see that there were armed men in it. She ran back to the Eagle house. Brave Warrior was standing in the archway of the totem pole with a bow and arrow.

"Did Will and Fox-of-the-Water come back?" she asked him.

"No," the Indian boy's father said. "I came out to watch for them. Go into the house, Mandy. It's not safe for you here."

Amanda was older than either of the boys. She was not going to leave them in danger. She ran toward the next house.

"Mandy, come back!" Brave Warrior called. Amanda kept on running.

When she came to the third house, she saw a man in wooden armor just inside the door. Will and Fox-of-the-Water must have awakened the people here.

The next house showed signs of life, too, but the last two houses were still quiet. Amanda was about to enter the fifth house when someone ran out and almost knocked her over.

"Mandy! What are you doing here?"
It was Will.

"Where's Fox-of-the-Water?" Amanda
asked.

"In the last house," her brother told
her. "He said the people there sleep
like logs. Come on. Let's help him wake
them up."

They reached the sixth house just as
the Indian boy was coming out. "Mandy,
you should be indoors!" He was excited.
"Let's get our bows and arrows, Will!"

Amanda looked around. She pointed
at the bay. By now the great canoe was
in shallow water. Most of the men who
came in it were wading ashore.

The children were standing in a patch
of moonlight.

"Get down!" Fox-of-the-Water dropped
to the ground and slid on his stomach
to the shadow of the nearest house. Will
and Amanda did the same.

As soon as they were out of the moonlight, the three of them stood up and stayed close to the wall of the house.

The men in the boat must have hoped to surprise the little village and capture people while they were still asleep or, at least, unarmed. They formed six groups and came quietly ashore. Each group crept toward a house.

The men of the village in their wooden armor waited in the shadows of their doorways. When the attackers came close they shot them with arrows and rushed at them with spears and clubs.

Many of the strangers fell to the ground. Some were killed. Others were badly hurt. Those who could still run went back to the canoe.

The people in the sixth and last house had only just been awakened. They were not as well prepared as the others.

The attackers did not manage to get into this house, either, but they were not badly hurt. When they saw their friends running back to the boat, they decided to follow them. Then one caught sight of Amanda and the boys hiding in the shadows. He made a signal.

The children were grabbed by three strong men and dragged to the big canoe.

26

THE strange men threw Amanda and the boys into the canoe. They pushed it into deeper water, climbed in, and began to paddle.

The children huddled together on the bottom of the boat. No one bothered with them. Many of the men were bleeding and crippled from the fighting. The others were paddling as hard as they could. There seemed to be a lot of people here, but Amanda couldn't make out their faces in the dark.

She looked over the side of the canoe. "We have to get out of here before we're any farther away from shore. Jump, Fox-of-the-Water!"

The Indian boy shook his head. "The land otter people would own my soul forever!"

Amanda could see there was no use arguing with him. She jabbed her elbow into her brother's ribs and cocked her head toward the water. "Heave-ho, Will!" she whispered.

Amanda grabbed Fox-of-the-Water by the shoulders and Will lifted his feet off the ground. Together they threw the young Indian overboard. Then they dived after him into the dark waters of the bay.

The men in the boat heard the noise as the children hit the water. They saw that their captives were missing, but they went on paddling.

Fox-of-the-Water landed with a splash. Then he sank. Amanda and Will dived down after their friend and pulled him to the surface.

"Remember what we told you about treading water?" Amanda said. "That's what I'm doing now." She held his head above water.

"If you get tired, roll over and swim on your back." Will swam in a lazy circle around his sister and Fox-of-the-Water. "And don't forget to kick like a frog."

Before long all three children were swimming toward shore. No lights were burning in the village houses to guide them. They swam in the other direction from the mountain in hopes of reaching their own beach.

All three were very tired when at last they staggered out of the surf onto the sand.

Amanda just wanted to curl up and go to sleep on the beach, but Fox-of-the-Water insisted that they had to run up and down the beach to warm up.

They played a game of tag in the moonlight. Then they dug three holes in the sand above the high-water mark. The children lay down and covered themselves with sand to wait for morning. Long before the sun came up they were asleep.

27

AMANDA was the first to open her eyes. She sat up and stretched. Then she went to wake up the boys.

All three of the children were hungry. The beach was covered with oysters. Neither Amanda nor Will had ever tasted them, but they had watched their father eat them on the half shell.

Fox-of-the-Water told them he never got as many oysters as he wanted. All the other people in his uncle's house liked them just as much as he did.

He opened an oyster with his knife and smelled it. "Fresh!" The Indian boy held out the oyster. "You can have the first one, Mandy."

To her surprise, Amanda found that the oyster had a delicate, cool, salty taste. "Will, you don't know what you're missing!"

They feasted on oysters for breakfast and finished the meal with wild strawberries that were growing at the edge of the wood.

Fox-of-the-Water first looked at the mountain across the bay. Then he looked at the sun. He turned to the right and started walking along the beach.

Will and Amanda hurried after him.

They walked steadily for two hours. When they rounded a curve in the bay, they saw the village. The first house they came to was the one where they had been captured the night before.

Fox-of-the-Water started to run. Amanda and Will were right behind him. They raced along the beach till they came to the totem pole with the eagle on top.

All the people from the house were outdoors facing the water, but no one was singing.

The Indian boy rushed to his mother. She bent down and hugged him. Her face was wet with tears.

For a little while no one spoke. Then Mountain Echo said, "We were told that you were carried away in the enemy canoe."

"We were," Will told him, "but we jumped out of the boat and swam ashore."

At this everybody seemed to step back, as if to move away from the children.

Sunset Moon looked frightened. She hugged her son tighter.

Fox-of-the-Water looked at his mother. Then he fainted. Sunset Moon laid him gently on the sand.

"Isn't anybody going to do anything for him?" Amanda cried.

"The only one who could do anything would be the saya-gay," Brave Warrior told her. "We haven't seen Bright Star today. He may be dead."

"I'm going to get him," Amanda turned to run.

"Take care, Mandy," Brave Warrior warned. "The spirit of a saya-gay is an evil thing!"

28

AMANDA started to run toward the little house of the saya-gay.

"Wait for me, Mandy." Will came after her.

The mat was hanging over the doorway again. Will and Amanda could hear the same scraping sound Amanda had heard before. She called, "Bright Star, come quickly before Fox-of-the-Water dies!"

The noise stopped. "What's wrong with the boy?" the saya-gay asked from the other side of the mat.

"The land otter spirits have taken his soul," Will said. "It's our fault. We threw him out of the enemy canoe into the water last night!"

Bright Star lifted the mat and came out. "I didn't know there had been a raid!" he said. "I've been working day and night to polish that rock you gave me.

"Will, I'll need you to help me set up these." He dragged some carved and painted cedarwood planks from behind his house. "Mandy, go back and tell Mountain Echo and Brave Warrior to bring Fox-of-the-Water here at once. Hurry!"

Amanda ran back with the message.

Fox-of-the-Water was awake now. He seemed to know what was going on, but he couldn't speak.

Amanda held the Indian boy's hand and led him to the saya-gay's house. His mother and father and uncle followed them. All the other people who lived in Mountain Echo's house came after.

Bright Star made Amanda and Will sit beside Fox-of-the-Water on the platform in front of his house. He told them to be very quiet. The painted boards had been set up on the platform to look like a boat.

The other people stood around and watched as if they were in a theater. They seemed to Amanda like small children who thought everything they saw on the stage was real.

The saya-gay got into his magic boat. It took him to the underworld. There he fought with a ghost in a spooky battle. He came back with the soul of Amanda in his hands. He placed the invisible soul on her head. "Go and join the healthy people," he commanded.

Amanda went to stand beside Sunset Moon, who bent down to kiss her.

Bright Star paddled back to the underworld to fight another ghost. This time he brought back Will's soul, and Will went to join his sister.

The last voyage was longer. Waves nearly wrecked the magic boat. The watching people held their breath.

The third ghost was meaner and harder to outwit. The saya-gay fell to the ground more than once. At last, weary but still brave, Bright Star tenderly placed Fox-of-the-Water's soul on the Indian boy's head. "You are well now," the saya-gay said.

Fox-of-the-Water stood up. "I am forever grateful to you, Bright Star."

The people cheered.

29

AMANDA was helping Sunset Moon heat stones to drop into the wooden boxes of water. "Where is the slave woman?" she asked.

"She must have sneaked out of the side door and gone off with our enemies last night," Sunset Moon said. "Several of the slaves are missing. Perhaps they thought some of the raiders were members of their clans."

Amanda said nothing. She was happy for the slaves.

"Brave Warrior and I have been talking." Sunset Moon picked up a stone with a pair of wooden tongs. "You saved our village. We are going to adopt you and Will and change your names. Fox-of-the-Water needs a brother, and you will be the daughter I have always wanted."

For a minute Amanda was silent. Then she said, "I'd better go and tell Will."

Amanda ran across the beach to where her brother was skipping stones into the bay. She told him what Sunset Moon had said. "I guess we ought to be grateful. I don't want to hurt anyone's feelings, but I miss Mom and Dad!" Amanda was almost crying.

"I feel the same way." Will dropped the stone he was holding. "Let's go talk to Bright Star."

They ran as fast as they could to the saya-gay's house. He was not there.

Amanda pointed farther down the beach. "I think I see him."

Bright Star was standing near the wooden statue where Will and Amanda first found themselves when they looked up from the black mirror.

When he saw the two children, the witch doctor called to them. "Come here. I've something to show you."

"Why the rush?" Will asked.

"Don't ask questions!" the saya-gay told him. "I've done the best I could with this thing, and I don't want anyone to see it but you two. If it works, I'll bury it in the sand." He walked away from the statue.

Amanda saw the black rock where the saya-gay had placed it, flat in the sand at the base of the statue. She pulled Will over to it. Bright Star had polished the stone until it gleamed in the sunlight.

They looked down to see the statue dimly reflected in the stone. The bright colors were gone. The wood looked old and battered, and the blue sky above it didn't show at all.

Suddenly both Amanda and Will had the same wild hope. Maybe Bright Star's black mirror was *magic!*

They looked up to find themselves once again in the Brooklyn Museum!

The guard came walking over to them. "You're not old enough to be allowed in here without a grown-up. Who knows what might happen to you?"

"I'm sorry," Amanda said. "We didn't know it was against the rules."

They went out into the heat of the afternoon.

Will grinned. "At least we went swimming."

Amanda grinned, too.

Other books by Ruth Chew

The Wednesday Witch
Baked Beans for Breakfast
(also known as *The Secret Summer*)
No Such Thing as a Witch
Magic in the Park
What the Witch Left
The Hidden Cave
(in hardcover as *The Magic Cave*)
The Witch's Buttons
The Secret Tree House
The Would-Be Witch
Witch in the House
The Trouble with Magic
Summer Magic
Witch's Broom
The Witch's Garden
Earthstar Magic
The Wishing Tree
Second-hand Magic
Mostly Magic
The Magic Coin
The Witch at the Window
Trapped in Time
Do-It-Yourself Magic
The Witch and the Ring